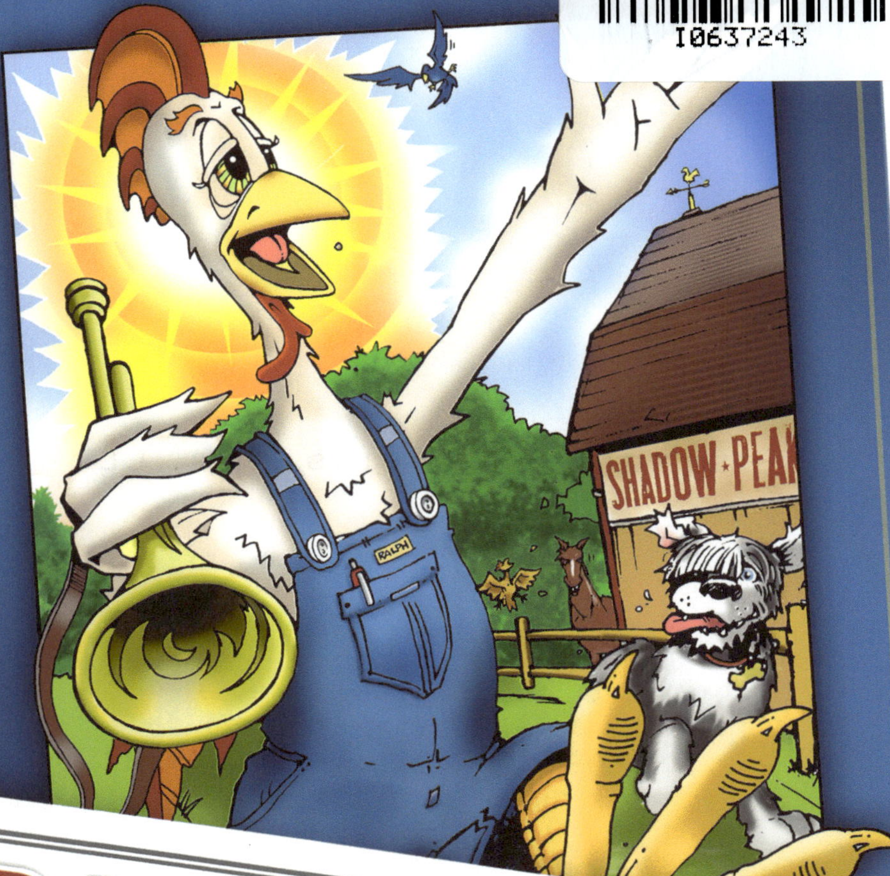

RALPH'S BUGLE

★ BETTER DAY PUBLISHING ★

THE CROW HEARD ROUND THE WORLD!

Written by

Naresha S. Perry

Illustrated by Todd Pearl

BETTER DAY PUBLISHING, LLC

ISBN 978-0-9767189-2-5

©2010 Better Day Publishing, LLC

3695F Cascade Road, #2161
Atlanta, GA 30331

Printed in the USA.

DEDICATION

This book is dedicated to my family and friends who have encouraged me along the way.

Thanks for your continued support!

Love,

Naresha

The legacy of Wake Master originated centuries ago, as farmers grew more reliant upon one species of animal for the survival of their existence – the mighty crowing rooster.

The Wake Master's position grew to be one of prestige and honor, as farms flourished throughout the world – This was due to the rooster's mighty crow.

The Wake Master's call can be heard throughout many lands today...

"Er-er-er-er-errrrr!" crowed Old Simon Le Bell. "Er-er-er-er-errrr!" as the sun crept above the hills. Ralph, the young rooster sat wondering how long it would be before he would reign as "Wake Master" of Shadow Peak Farm.

"Listen, sonny boy," warned Old Simon Le Bell. "It takes a well trained, disciplined soldier to carry out the duties of Wake Master." Old Simon Le Bell chattered on. "It doesn't hurt to have well developed lungs either. My father was Wake Master, his father and of course, Moí. Now, my days as Wake Master are numbered. That means you, my boy, must step up to the plate. Wake Master has a very important job to do. He is the heartbeat of the farm – the timekeeper. If he snoozes a second too long, he might as well pack his things.

3

There's no coming back after such a catastrophe!
The last soldier ousted from this position was Sir
Call'um, in 1929. His two seconds of sleep cost us
months of overtime labor, and widespread famine.
It was the most dreaded time this great farm has
ever seen! Our motto since that great disaster has
been to 'Snooze Light! Crow with Might!' Shadow
Peak hasn't seen such a disaster since!"

Alarmed by Old Simon Le Bell's warning, Ralph began to doubt. "What if I don't succeed? What if I oversleep? Don't crow loud enough? I don't want to fail." He thought to himself. Ralph paced anxiously. "Snooze Light! Crow with Might! Snooze Light! Crow with Might!" He repeated. "Snooze... I got it!" Ralph scurried to his secret trunk.

Ralph kept strange things in his trunk. Among them were one wool army- green sock, an aged alarm clock, and a ratty old bugle. Ralph pulled the old bugle from the heap. "Thrrrrr-r-thr-thr!" The old bugle sounded. There's no way anyone can sleep through this! I'll set my clock 5 minutes earlier. That way I'll wake everyone up on time.

It was the first morning of Ralph's duty as Wake Master. Ralph's alarm chimed at approximately 5:55 A.M. Ralph grabbed his bugle, then darted for the bedroom window of the farmer's house. "Thr-thr-thr-thr-thrrrr!" Violently awaking the humans, and blowing as loudly as he could, Ralph headed for the chicken coop, "Thr-thr-thr-thr-thrrrr!" sending the hens into a scurry of madness.

Ralph darted for the horse's stables, "Thr-thr-thr-thr-thrrrr!" jolting Hooch, and the rest of the horses from their restful state. Rounding out his timed route – Ralph flew past the pig's pen, the cow's meadow, and the goat's territory, "Thr-thr-thr-thr-thrrrr!" "What in heaven's name is that!" shrieked Geech the goat, seeing only a flash of feathers and a bugle. Ralph had successfully completed his first day as Wake Master. Everyone was shaken but awake. The farm was alive and kicking. Chickens laid eggs, cows produced milk, mules plowed the fields, and farmers made profits.

The alarmed sounded the second day of Ralph's duty as Wake Master. Ralph grabbed his bugle, then began his route. Hurrying toward the farmer's bedroom window - he blew, "Thr-thr-thr-thr-thrrrr!"
Then sprinting to the door of the chicken coop, "Thr-thr-thr-thr-thrrrr!" Speeding towards the horse's stables, Ralph blew, "Thr-thr-thr-thr-thrrrr!"

11

"What is that horrible noise!" grumbled Murle the old mule. "It's the young rooster Ralph," yawned Naomi the cow. "Why doesn't he just crow for goodness sake!" crabbed Murle. "Thr-thr-thr-thr-thrrrr!" Ralph blew as hard and loudly as he could, barreling past the pig's pen, the cow's meadow, and the goat's territory.

Again, the farm bustled with animals and farmers. By the end of the week the farmer obtained double his income. The mules plowed 50% more land.

The cows produced 50% more milk. The chickens laid 50% more eggs. However, the animals were not happy.

"My ears are ringing from that gawd awful thing he blows every morning!" complained Murle. "I have a nervous twitch now," wined Polo the pig. "There's got to be something we can do!' "I suggest cotton. Place it in your ears. Maybe it will ease the ringing," suggested Naomi. "That won't work!" griped Murle. "It's just a suggestion." Naomi countered, swaying off from the group now gathering at the white wooden fence of the farm.

Hooch the horse and Sam the shepherd dog were approaching. "What's the commotion about?" questioned Sam. "It's that bugle and that renegade rooster!" fumed Geech the goat. "He's out of hand!" added Polo the pig.

"Leave him alone. He's only doing his job," defended Hooch the horse. "It's easy for you to say. You're not rudely awakened by his racket!" grumbled Geech the goat. "Hey! We've gotten more done this week than we have in months," reasoned Naomi. "Yeah, leave the young chap alone! He's doing the best he can," added Hooch the horse. "Fine. But I'll be deaf before I'm old!" conceded Polo the pig.

Later that night Polo, Geech, and Murle met back at the old wooden gate. "We've got to do something about that rooster's bugle." Murle complained. "I have an idea. Let's get Richie the raccoon to help us," plotted Geech. "You mean have him steal it?" yelled Polo. Quickly covering Polo's mouth, "Shhhh- pipe down!" Geech warned. "Yes. If we pay him handsomely, our troubles will be over." "Sounds good, but where are we going to find him?" muffled Polo through Geech's hoof. "When Sly the fox makes his nightly trek through the fields, we'll ask him to relay a message."

Just like clock work, there appeared Sly dragging a bag of stolen goods. Some poor farmer's coop had been violated. "Psst." Sly stopped in his tracks without looking around. He waited. "Psst.... Sly!"

Geech summoned. "I didn' doow it!" Confessed Sly, with his hands raised. "Shhh! It's me Geech." "Oh! Hiya dere." "Do you happen to know where we can find Richie?" "Uh-Richie? Yeh. Whaddaya wan wit em?" "We have a job for him. Think you can get a message to him?" asked Polo. "Uh. Yeh. What's da messige?" "Tell him to meet Polo and Geech at the north gate, at nightfall tomorrow." "Nort gate, Nightfawl. – Uh. What's in it for me?" propositioned Sly. "We'll tell you later. Just get the message to Richie," warned Murle the mule. Sly was not a confrontational fox. He shrugged, then slinked off with his goods.

The next day, Ralph set out on his route. As usual, the farm was bursting with industry, and as usual Polo and other animals complained about Ralph and his

bugle. At nightfall, Sly, Richie, Polo, and Geech met at the north gate of Shadow Peak Farm. Geech and Polo had drawn up a proposal, then simply handed it over to Richie. Silently he read it, pulled out his pen, jotted down a quote, then handed it over to Geech and Polo. Geech then pulled out his pen, jotted down a compromise, then handed it back to Rich. Rich and Sly stole off for a moment, returned, and nodded in agreement to Geech and Polo's proposal. "He keeps the bugle in a suitcase under his bed." Geech whispered. Sly and Richie nodded and crept away.

As it turns out, Geech and Polo ultimately agreed to pay Sly and Richie $300.00. However, Sly and Richie had other plans. Their plan was to kidnap 2 chickens, 2 lambs, and a dozen eggs for chicken soup, lamb chops, and scrambled eggs. They figured that the winter holidays were approaching. It would be easier to get full on free food, and use the cash for future barter and trade.

Sly and Richie snuck to a nearby pasture, where they planned their scheme. They would arrive at the west gate of Shadow Peak Farm at 5:30 A. M. There was a  large maple tree. Using a rope tied around Richie's waste, Richie would secure the bugle, then tug twice to be lifted. Once the bugle was secured, Sly and Richie would kidnap Lady Cal and Old Simon Le Bell. They would then go to the sheep's pen to kidnap 2 of the youngest of the sheep herd. This was their plan.

It was 5:30 A.M. Sly and Richie were in place at the top of the maple tree. Sly lowered Richie into the chicken coop over Ralph's bed. Just as Richie's paws touched the floor, Ralph rustled. Richie stood as still as he could. Ralph's breathing was slow

and deep. He was sleeping soundly. Richie managed to reach the suitcase, and secured the bugle.

Tugging twice on the rope, he was hoisted back into the tree. It was now 5:40 A.M. Richie and Sly made their way over to the chicken coop, where they grabbed Lady Cal and Old Simon Le Bell. Grabbing, then taping their beaks and wings first made their job easier.

Sly and Richie stuffed the two birds into the bag, and 2-dozen eggs from the bend. Their clocks showed 5:45 A.M. They were headed to the sheep's pen when Ralph's alarm sounded. His clock showed 5:55 A.M. Ralph began to scramble, searching for his bugle. It wasn't in the suitcase! Ralph immediately knew something was wrong.

He jostled over to the chicken coop, where he noticed Lady Cal's and Old Simon Le Bell's beds were empty. Ralph began to crow in fright. "ER-ER-ER-ER-ERRRR! ER-ER-ER-ER-ERRRRR! We've been robbed! ER-ER-ER-ER-ERRRR!" It was a loud and hearty crow. Running from the chicken coop to the farmer's window, Ralph crowed. "ER-ER-ER-ER-ERRRR!" As he rounded the corner of the horse's stalls, Ralph spotted the culprits. Richie and Sly were stuffing sheep into their bags when Ralph, Sam, and the farmer came charging toward them. "ER-ER-ER-ER-ER-ERRRR! Stop thieves!"

ERRRR!

Sly and Richie darted towards the white fence, clearing it. They sprinted across the fields of Cows Feet County. Ralph crowed louder. "ER-ER-ER-ER-ERRRR!" It was now 6:00 A.M. The sun had begun to creep across the sky. Ralph's crowing could be heard many miles away.

Animals and farmers from Chicken Pock County to Measly County were fast at work.

Meanwhile, the chase was on. Ralph and Sam gained speed, closing the distance left by Sly and Richie. They crossed creeks and hills,

as the chase continued. Ralph's loud crows echoed across the valleys and hills of Cracked Corn County, and even further. "ER-ER-ER-ER-ERRRR!" Just as Sly and Richie darted around the corner of a nearby barn, out shot Hooch the horse. Staring them down with his sturdy brown eyes, Hooch warned. "Make one more move and I will crush your skinny necks!" Murle and Hooch were now towering over Sly and Richie. Neither Sly nor Richie moved. Ralph and Sam had just zoomed passed as they caught sight of Sly and the others. Lady Cal and Old Simon Le Bell's muffled cries for help could be heard from inside the big bag Sly hid behind his back. With a slinky grin on his face, Sly tightened his grip. "Let them go!"

demanded Murle as he charged for Sly, trampling
him. The bag was knocked from Sly's hands. Lady
Cal and Old Simon Le Bell tumbled from the bag,
along with Ralph's bugle. The farmer snatched Sly
and Richie up by the necks. "Gotcha!" He yelled.
The chase was over.

CITY NEWS

MAY 3, 2010

ARD ROUND THE WORLD!

YOUNG RALPH CHOSEN AS NEW REGIONAL WAKE MASTER

The mayor inaugurated Ralph as Region Wake Master. He has been given charge of 10 counties to be exact. These include all the counties from Shadow Peak to Cracked Corn County. In addition to that, Ralph was awarded the key to Capital City.

K TO CRACKED CORN
SAVE THE REGION

Farms from surrounding counties, from Shadow Peak to Cracked Corn County have all netted profits. Ranging from the 50-75 percent, the surrounding counties are no longer in debt! Farmers have paid all their bills and now they and their families sleep comfortably at night. It is all because of the brave rooster's mighty crow!

SHADOW PEAK FARMS

PRODUCTION UP 50%

In the first week of Ralph's reign as Wake Master, Shadow Peak farm obtained double its income. The mules plowed 50% more land. The cows produced 50% more milk and the chickens laid 50% more eggs. This is unbelievable!

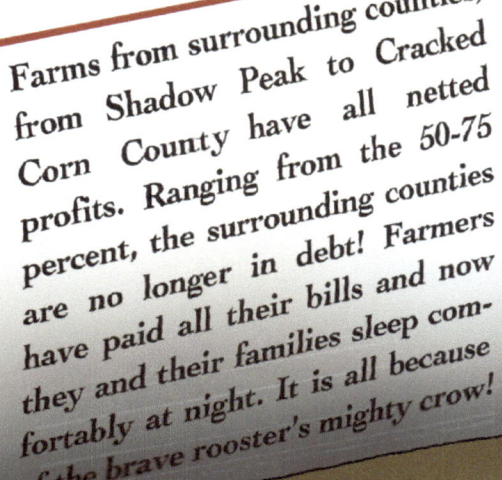

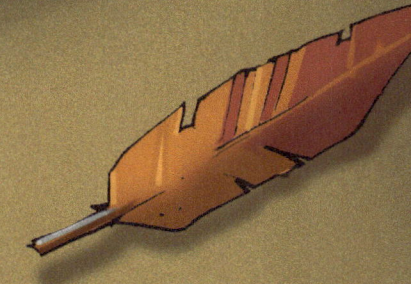

It was later revealed that Sly and Richie had victimized every farm from Shadow Peak to Macon Valley. They were locked away, and never heard from again. Soon after, other farm animals talked of how brave Ralph was, and the mighty crow he emitted during the chase. The talk of Ralph's mighty crow had made its way to the mayor's office. News was traveling fast. Farms from surrounding counties had produced 50 percent more in that day than any other. With all the farmers netting profits ranging from 50-75 percent or more, the surrounding counties were no longer in debt. Farmers could pay bills, and sleep comfortably at night. They had no more worries. It was all because of the brave rooster's mighty crow. It awakened farm animals miles and miles away, 15-30 minutes before their normal time. Those few minutes saved the entire region from bankruptcy.

As it turns out, the mayor inaugurated Ralph as Region Wake Master. This meant he was given charge of every farm from Shadow Peak to Cracked Corn County – 10 counties to be exact. In addition to that, Ralph was awarded the key to Capital City.

Ralph, overwhelmed with joy, made the most profound speech. "I accept the duties of Region Wake Master with honor. Unfortunately, I doubted myself, and my ability to carry out the duties of Wake Master. I doubted because I didn't know the gift that lay inside of me. Now, I know that I had it all along. I just

needed to believe in myself! From this day forth, I promise to carry out the duties of Region Wake Master with pride and confidence!" The cheers of the farmers, and farm animals filled the streets of Capital City.

Later, the farm animals confessed and apologized to Ralph for plotting to steal his bugle. He willingly forgave his farm mates. Soon, the whole nasty matter was forgotten. Ralph continues his rein as Region Wake Master to this very day. If you listen closely, Ralph's mighty crow can be heard in your town, too!

RALPH'S BUGLE
DOUBLE PUZZLE

CITPULR

DETTEMI

REORSOT

LEGBU

TISHO

TEOSTDP

BERTAR

SECREU

RAPHL

LYS

W K

Unscramble each of the clue words.

Take the letters that appear in ⬭ boxes and unscramble them for the final message.

RALPH'S BUGLE
Maze through Cracked Corn County

RALPH'S BUGLE WORD FIND

```
Y T I R P L U C O S
R E V H Y G E E C H
E L C T Y Y Y K E R
T G R S C J Y R M E
R U A I P L U X I T
A B L O S C W R T S
B Y P H E O R B T O
N Q H S Z V Z B E O
A G J G F Y Y A D R
G X D E T T O P S D
```

SECURE   ROOSTER   SPOTTED

HOIST   CULPRIT   EMITTED

BARTER   SLY   RALPH

BUGLE   GEECH

ORDER MORE BETTER DAY TITLES

Titles:

Zora's Valentine	(978-0-9767189-0-1)	$15.00
Calvin Didn't Know	(978-9767189-3-2)	$15.00
Ralph's Bugle	(978-9767189-2-5)	$15.00
The Chocolate Moose	(978-9767189-5-6)	$15.00
Nobody Told Jamaal	(978-0-9796763-9-0)	$15.00

Shipping Address

City   State   Zip Code

Contact Person   Phone

Payment Method:

☐ Visa   ☐ Master Card   ☐ Money Order

Credit Card Number   Exp. Date

Card Holders Signature

ISBN #	Book Title	Quantity	Price	Shipping	Total
				Grand Total	

Mail to:
Better Day Publishing, LLC
3695F Cascade Road, #2161
Atlanta, GA 30331
www.betterdaypublishing.com

"Bridging Minds to Better Days"

The Illustrator

Todd Pearl is an accomplished freelance illustrator and designer who happens to be Creative Director and illustrator for Better Day Publishing. He has illustrated many children's books, and currently working on one of his own. Todd resides in Clawson, MI, just outside of Detroit with his wife, Lisa and their two dachshunds, Stella and Cooper. View Todd's work at **www.toddpearl.com**

BETTER DAY PUBLISHING, LLC